A MESSAGE TO PARENTS

It is of vital importance for parents to read good books to young children in order to aid the child's psychological and intellectual development. At the same time as stimulating the child's imagination and awareness of his environment, it creates a positive relationship between parent and child. The child will gradually increase his basic vocabulary and will soon be able to read books alone.

Brown Watson has published this series of books with these aims in mind. By collecting this inexpensive library, parent and child are provided with hours of pleasurable and profitable reading.

The Ugly Duckling

Text by Maureen Spurgeon

ENGLAND

Mother Duck had found the perfect place on the farm to build her nest. It was cool and dry, with plenty of grass, yet close enough to a stream when the time came to take her ducklings for a swim. The other ducks quacked and splashed about in the water, as she sat waiting for her eggs to hatch.

Then, at last, came the great day when the shells burst open, one after the other!

"Cheep-Cheep!" piped the tiny, yellow ducklings as they waddled around. "How wide the world is!"

Mother Duck fussed round them
proudly. She was so busy trying to
keep all her ducklings together,
that, at first, she did not notice
there was one egg, bigger than
any of the others, still in the nest.

"That's a turkey's egg!" quacked
an old duck when she saw it.
"And turkeys never learn to swim,
my dear, not like our little ones.
Nasty birds, they are, too! Take
my advice and leave it alone."

But Mother Duck said she would sit on the egg a little longer until it hatched. And, instead of a pretty, yellow duckling, out came a fat, ugly chick with horrible dark grey feathers!

"Was this a turkey chick?" wondered Mother Duck, leading the way down to the stream. How glad she was to see the ugly little bird swimming along behind the others.

"He's not a turkey," she thought, "just an Ugly Duckling."
The Ugly Duckling soon began to grow, and as he grew, the uglier he became. The other ducklings wouldn't even talk to him.

The hens in the farmyard pecked at him whenever he came near. Worst of all was the turkey cock who came at the Ugly Duckling making loud gobbling noises, until it was red in the face.

Even the little girl who fed the farmyard birds aimed kicks at him. Unhappy and frightened, he flew off, some smaller birds getting out of his way. "That's because I'm so ugly," he thought.

The Ugly Duckling flew on until
he came to a marsh where some
wild ducks lived.
"My," said one, "you're so ugly!"
The Ugly Duckling just fluffed up
his feathers and fell asleep.

Next day, the air was shattered by hunters shooting at the wild ducks. The Ugly Duckling thought he would die when one of the dogs found him. Then – splash – the dog turned and went.

"I'm so ugly!" thought the Ugly Duckling. "Even the dog does not bite me." And he went on his way, until he came to a hut where an old woman lived with her cat and a hen. Nobody saw him creeping inside . . .

The woman thought the Ugly Duckling was a lady duck to lay eggs for her. But as he grew fatter and uglier and no eggs came, she got angry. The hen and cat hated him because he could swim.

All summer long the Ugly Duckling was all alone, eating whatever he could find. Then came the autumn when the leaves blew down from the trees and the clouds hung low in the sky.

Then at sunset one day, the Ugly Duckling saw the most beautiful white birds flying across the lake. He watched them until they were out of sight, wishing with all his heart that he could be with them.

The winter snow reminded him of those beautiful white birds. The river froze, almost freezing the Ugly Duckling with it, until a kind man broke the ice and took him home.

His children wanted to play, but the Ugly Duckling thought they would hurt him. They scared him so much that he splashed into a pail of milk, and then into a barrel of oatmeal!

The children laughed and laughed, but their mother was furious. The Ugly Duckling only just missed being hit by the fire tongs, as he ran out into the bitter winter weather.

Now came the worst part of the Ugly Duckling's whole life. Often he felt he would die from hunger and cold, longing for some shelter. He could hardly believe it when the sun shone again, and birds sang.

Hearing the birds, the Ugly Duckling flapped his wings, surprised to find how big and strong they had become. The sun warmed his back as he flew,

making him feel happier than he had been for a long, long time.

On and on flew the Ugly Duckling until he saw a garden, the scent of flowers wafting up towards him. Suddenly, three beautiful white swans flew out from the thicket, gliding into the water.

These were the birds he had seen in the autumn, the ones he loved – although he did not know why. "What if they hurt me?" he thought. "Better to die here than to be beaten and punished because I'm so ugly . . ."

Slowly, the swans turned and came towards him, looking so solemn that the Ugly Duckling bowed his head. He saw his reflection in the water – not the reflection of an Ugly Duckling but of a beautiful white swan.

The Ugly Duckling thought he was dreaming! Could he really be a beautiful swan?
"There's a new swan! Isn't he lovely?" said some little children as they stood by the lake .